FACES OF CARTERVILLE

FACES OF CARTERVILLE

A HENRY CARTER MYSTERY

ROBERT J. MCCARTER

LITTLE HUMMINGBIRD PUBLISHING

Faces of Carterville

A Henry Carter Mystery

Copyright © 2024 by Robert J. McCarter

Except as permitted under the Copyright Act of 1976, this book may not be reproduced in whole or in part in any manner.

This book is a work of fiction. Names, places, and incidents are either products of the author's imagination or used fictitiously. Any resemblance to actual events or persons, living or dead, is entirely coincidental.

Cover image © Robert J. McCarter

Version 1.0, July 2024

ISBN: 978-1-963354-09-6

Visit Robert's website at: www.RobertJMcCarter.com

Published by:

Little Hummingbird Publishing

P.O. Box 23518

Flagstaff, AZ 86002

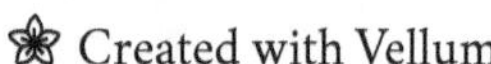 Created with Vellum

- **Out of a Christmas Sky**
- **Destroyer of Carterville**
- **The Blood of Carterville**
- **Faces of Carterville**
- **Return to Carterville**

Note: The events of this story take place nine months after *The Blood of Carterville*.

All the previous Carterville stories, *Out of a Christmas Sky*, *Destroyer of Carterville*, and *The Blood of Carterville*, were stand-alone containing only implicit spoilers of the previous books.

This book is different. In it, Henry reflects on the incidents described in the other three books and it contains many explicit spoilers.

This book, by its very nature, also has one other significant difference: it does not take place in Carterville, thus the change in subtitle from "A Carterville Mystery" to "A Henry Carter Mystery."

ONE

Patty Walsh is still beautiful.

I don't understand why the thought was so loud in my head, reverberating like a bell. Of course, Patty is still beautiful. She has always been beautiful, inside and out, at least to me. And just because it had been nine months since I had seen her, since we had both left Carterville, Arizona, there was no reason that should change.

She still had curly red hair cascading down past her shoulders and bright green eyes. She still had those intriguing curves God had given her and the slowly invading grey and wrinkles her five decades on this planet had earned her. She wasn't one to hide her age and that just made her even more appealing.

As I sat across from her at a small table in a little coffee shop, I felt like a teenage boy who was worried his crush had somehow changed over the summer and was relieved to see that she hadn't, that she had only become more appealing.

Given that we were both no longer in Carterville and both without our powers, this was actually a valid concern. Clearly I find Patty physically attractive, but it was always more than that. She was empathetic and kind, creative and fun to be around, but how much of that had to do with her powers? How much of it was about the strange nature of Carterville itself?

Seeing her now, the question of whether she was attractive outside of Carterville without her powers had been answered with a resounding 'yes.'

But it was even more than that. I had left Carterville before she had, driven out by a conspiracy that used my own power against me, and some regrettable things had happened.

My eyes lingered on Patty's neck. No, I don't have a weird neck fetish. It was because she had been wearing a scarf around her neck the last time I saw her, and with good reason. She wasn't now and I breathed a little sigh of relief.

That conspiracy to get me out of Carterville included someone using their powers on me to force me to choke Patty. If their plan had worked, I would have killed her and then killed myself.

I almost reached up and touched the right side of my face to feel three thin scars from when Patty had been forced to scratch me during that same terrible night. I don't really mind that the signs of that struggle linger on my face, but I was so glad she bore no scars. Visible, at least.

"You look good, Henry," she said with a shy smile before quickly looking down and taking a sip of her coffee.

Looking at me and those scars had to be complicated for her. I couldn't resist and touched the scars on my face. My feelings about them are complicated, the worst of it being that every time I look in the mirror, I remember my hands around Patty's throat and all that was done to get me out of town.

She looked back up and her green eyes were intense. There was a need there, but I was pretty sure it wasn't the need my boyish crush wanted.

"You look good too, Patty," I said. She looked like she was going to look down again, but she held my gaze, nodded, and gave a pursed-lip smile.

"You lost weight," she said.

I shrugged and said, "I think it's the camping. And the walks. Just trying to sort it all out in my head."

She nodded. "There's a lot to sort out. I..." She bit her lip and looked away again.

The coffee shop was in a strip mall in the newer part of Pagosa Springs, Colorado, that is called "Uptown." It was modern and comfortable with a few couches in one corner and the near constant hissing of the espresso machine as it got its morning workout. The air was perfumed with the scent of coffee and sweets which was mostly lost on me given the company I was keeping.

It wasn't the rustic Carterville Diner, but since Patty was here, and asked me to meet her, I was more than happy to be here.

"Just say it," I said gently. I wanted to reach across the table and touch her hand, but I knew that was inappropriate. What might have been between us had been destroyed that night when she gave me these scars and I choked her. "We've been through enough that you can tell me anything, Patty."

She nodded and took a deep breath. "You are writing about what happened and I'm glad. We all have to find our way through this. But... I..."

"It's too much," I offered. "I've been sending you the chapters as I write them, and it's too much."

She nodded, her green eyes reflecting a potent mix of sadness and compassion. "Most days it's better for me if I don't think too much about Carterville."

I nodded and felt my brow furrow. She had stopped at Carterville eight years ago after a bad divorce in Colorado. Carterville had been her haven, her place to heal. Hearing that it was hard to think about it felt like a punch to the stomach. Carterville, the town founded by my ancestor Samuel Carter, the town that bore my name, was now another place she had to escape from.

If you somehow missed all the news about it, Carterville, Arizona, is a town in Northern Arizona perched on the north side of the San Francisco Peaks. A struggling old mining town that was like so many out west until the meteor hit, until everyone in Carterville got powers. But those powers only work within about a five-mile radius from the center of town.

"No, no, Henry," she said, reaching across the table and grabbing my hand and squeezing it. "It's not that."

Her hand was warm and welcome, and I squeezed back. "It's not?" I asked. I didn't elaborate because this felt like the Carterville Patty, the one who had a power, the one with the empathic superpower and knew everything you wanted.

"It's not that night," she said, her eyes darting away for a moment. "If that was what you were thinking." She bit her lip and looked shy and awkward again.

I blinked, trying to understand. "What is it then?"

"My power," she said, letting go of my hand and staring at her coffee. "I used to know what everyone wanted. Most days it got to be too much, but I got used to it, I used it, probably too much. I'm still learning how to function without it."

"You can go back," I said quietly, not adding, "but I can't."

"No," she said, her fierce eyes meeting mine. "No. I can't."

She didn't elaborate and I didn't ask her to. There were so many reasons to stay away. The dynamics of a small town where almost everyone had powers, even though most were minor or quirky, were dangerous to say the least. And that night was a trauma, to be sure. Not to mention what happened during the whole "Destroyer of Carterville" mess.

There was more to talk about, to be sure—so much more and I hoped that we had time—but for now, I needed to change the subject.

"Why am I here, Patty?" I asked. "Your text was rather… vague." It was more than that. It said: *Please come visit. I have a problem. Can't discuss further unless we are in person.*

She sighed and gave me a shy smile. "I…" she said, looking around the coffee shop like she was afraid we would be over-head. Part of me got that. Pagosa Springs was not nearly as small as Carterville, but it was a small town and it's hard to keep your business private in small towns. "Well… I think it's best I show you."

TWO

Northern Arizona and Southern Colorado bear some striking similarities. Both are at around seven thousand feet in elevation, both are dominated by ponderosa pine trees, and both have their fair share of small mountain towns. The forest was different here, more scrub oak, no piñon or juniper, but the biggest differences were water and the mountains.

While Northern Arizona is dominated by one small mountain range with six peaks, the San Francisco Peaks, Southern Colorado is shaped by a vast range of mountains, the San Juan Mountains, with twenty-eight peaks over nine thousand feet. And there are rivers everywhere. The San Juan River runs through downtown Pagosa.

Overall, the feeling is very familiar and quite foreign at the same time. The land is fairly arid, they don't get much more rain here than we do in Northern Arizona, but the San Juans collect a lot of moisture which turns into the rivers that run through this land.

I had spent time in Colorado, of course, but seeing it with Patty made it clear why she had stopped at Carterville all those years ago when she was escaping Colorado. She had just come through a long expanse of dry desert and had gotten back into the pine trees. It must have reminded her of home.

"This is it," Patty said quietly. We had left my old pickup truck at the coffee shop, and she had driven through some winding roads north of Route 160, past lovely homes scattered over mountain meadows, past one lake, around another lake, and pulled into the driveway of a small log cabin perched on a large lake. The front of it was all garage with the house behind.

I was pretty sure the lakes were man-made, but there was so much water here I couldn't help but smile. Arizona is a desert, even when you are surrounded by pine trees, and this didn't feel like a desert.

Patty was just sitting in the driver's seat of her old-ish Prius, her hand gripping the steering wheel.

"Mind telling me what's going on, Patty?" I asked.

She looked at me and it was clear she was trying to find the words, so I continued, "I mean, I'm happy to go for a drive with you, happy to see this lovely neighborhood, and if that's all this is, fine by me. But it doesn't take powers to know something's going on."

She bit her lip and nodded. "You'll think I'm crazy."

"I don't think so," I said.

She gave a small laugh. "Oh, you are still you, aren't you?" she said.

"What?" I asked. I was confused.

"You didn't *promise* not to think I'm crazy," she said. "You know, like most people would do. Promise something that implies that they knew what the future holds, that they can actually keep the promise. But not you, not Henry Carter. You still aren't much for promises."

She was smiling and I couldn't help but smile back. There was pain and trauma reflected in our smiles, but they were smiles nonetheless so I'll take it.

"Not me," I said. "I don't have a clue about the future, that's for sure. And, as we both know, promises have power even when you aren't in Carterville."

In Carterville, the name I had been given by the media was "Promise Keeper." My power was, quite simply, the power of promises kept. If a promise was made to me or by me, it would be kept while near Carterville—no matter what.

When my best friend, Frank Paulson, was stabbed, I had promised Winston "Smitty" Smith that I would leave Carterville forever if he healed him and saved his life. It was my promise and my power that kept me from returning.

Patty nodded, the smile melting, and she took a deep breath. She glanced at the house in front of us and then back at me. "I… I know it doesn't make any sense, but… well… I think the house might be haunted."

I noticed that she said "the" house, not "my" house. Part of my brain, that part that had been a cop for more than two decades, was already working the case.

I looked up at the house. It was dark wood, an older house. When this area was built out, I'm sure it was houses like this on the lake that got built first.

It was kind of an odd house. There was no front door, or

front of the house, really. I had glimpsed a small window on the second floor as we turned in, but the front of the house was just garage. This is not the way you designed a house, so I figured the garage was newer, added on long after the house was built.

But it didn't look haunted. Not like you would see in the movies.

"Okay," I said with a gentle smile. "Run me through it. Why do you think this house is haunted?"

THREE

I was glad for the distraction, for Patty and me to be on a topic besides our past in Carterville. I'm not a big fan of mysteries, at least not when I'm trying to solve them. They are just fine on TV, but this was a mystery that let Patty and me spend time together, and for that I was grateful.

So, I watched her as we sat in her Prius in the driveway of "the" house and took in what she was telling me.

She had inherited the house from her uncle, a man that had no children and whose wife had died a few years earlier. She told me that houses on this lake, Lake Pagosa, didn't change hands very often and were coveted even if the houses were small and old like this one.

It was a little hard to focus at first.

I had been away from the job for a while now. My day used to be full of people telling me their problems and expecting me to do something about it. Back then, I always had a notebook in my back pocket and a cheap Bic pen and would always take notes.

But I had no notepad and no pen so I just watched Patty and listened.

And that was the other distraction. I had missed Patty and I had always enjoyed being in her presence, but being with her again made me feel like she was what I had been really missing since I left Carterville. Not the job. Not the town. But Patty.

I was old enough not to trust that thought. It was just the boyish crush getting the upper hand, but there was truth to it. We had been communicating since we both left, we were obviously friends, and we certainly couldn't be more, but I had clearly missed being near her.

"It was little things at first," she said. "Like strange flickering lights or voices I couldn't quite make out. Feeling like I'm being watched."

She stopped her monologue and stared at me. "You think I'm crazy," she said. It wasn't a question.

That boyish part of me wanted to say, "No, I think you're beautiful." But that's not what I said. I said, "No, I don't. You are experiencing something you can't explain. That doesn't make you crazy."

She nodded but didn't look convinced.

"Look, Patty," I said. "Carterville is not the only place where strange things happen. I'm here. I'm happy to help."

She nodded and then pursed her lips. "And there are big things that happen here," she said.

"Like what?" I asked.

"Doors," she said, her eyes flicking to the garage in front of us and the house.

I nodded at her to continue.

"They open," she said. "On their own. Specifically, the sliding glass door that opens on to the lake. I lock it at night, even put a stick in the track, and every week or so it's open when I get up. A couple of times it was wide open."

"Okay," I said. There was enough here that I should be writing things down. But I wasn't a cop anymore, was I? "Anything else 'big' happening?"

She nodded. "My paintings. They get rearranged. Some of them get turned upside down or so their back is facing out."

I really missed my notebook. Not because I couldn't remember what she was telling me but because it gave me something to do with my hands. Something to focus on besides who I was talking to.

Well, that often isn't an issue, but it was here. That boyish part of me was doing stupid backflips that Patty had reached out to me, that she wanted me to help her, so ergo she must want me.

Stupid brain.

"Maybe you should show me around," I said.

She nodded and rubbed her hands together nervously. "Okay."

Something was going on, but I was pretty sure Patty wasn't being haunted.

FOUR

The hardwood floors marked the age of the house. It wasn't laminate that looked like wood, it was real hardwood. Maybe maple.

Patty had driven us into the garage and the entrance to the house was two steps up, confirming my suspicion that the garage had been an add-on. This used to be the front door.

We walked down a hallway with a small bedroom to the right, a bathroom, and then it opened up with the kitchen to the right and the great room in front of us.

It was a small house. A simple house. All wood flooring with the back of the house, the part that faced Lake Pagosa, floor to vaulted ceiling glass.

To the right there was a staircase that went up to what looked like a loft bedroom.

You would think the view out those windows would steal the show. They faced east towards the lake with bumps of distant mountains on the horizon. Sunrise would be spectacular here, flooding the whole house with warm light.

But that's not what caught my attention. It was the paintings.

The room had a small couch and a flat-screen TV, but not much else in terms of furniture. All around me were paintings. Some hung, some on easels, at least ten paintings. Paintings of people. People I knew.

These were portraits, but some liberties had been taken. Maybe you would call them impressionistic. I don't know art well enough to say.

The faces were a little twisted or a little elongated, the colors not accurate, the proportions not quite right, but the overall effect was stunning.

The first one that caught my attention was a slim man with a sharp nose, green eyes, scraggly, greying blond hair, and several days' growth of beard.

"Smitty," I whispered, the painting clearly of Winston "Smitty" Smith. He had the power of healing, one of the true "super" powers in Carterville, and the promise I made to him was the reason I was unable to return home.

In the painting, Smitty's face was twisted, his jaw way too long, the face somehow looking old and adolescent at the same time, his eyes haunted and so vividly green it was a little disturbing. There was need in those eyes, a need that could never be met.

"You write," Patty said quietly behind me. "I paint."

I was writing to cope. Patty was painting to cope, and boy was she painting.

Annie Smith was featured on another canvas, the inside of the Carterville Inn in the background, Annie's arms crossed and her eyes glowing red, her high cheekbones overemphasized and her smile showing slightly sharpened canines.

The painting made Annie look like the epitome of jealousy, feral and dangerous. And I guess that was fair—it was her jealousy that got my expulsion from Carterville going.

The mayor of Carterville, Karen Winslow, was there. In her painting, Karen's hazel eyes were too wide, her mouth open way too far showing an empty unfillable void. Karen wanted Carterville to be a big deal and she wanted to own as much of it as possible. The painting laid her greed bare. While Karen hadn't actively participated in my ouster from Carterville, having me gone certainly served her purposes.

There were even more faces of Carterville: Martin Lester, Lila Chang, Frank and Lisa Paulson, Bo Larson, Lisa Bass, Mary and Thomas Reilly, and one more.

There was what looked to be a cowboy painted in profile with what was clearly the San Francisco Peaks rising in the background. His face wasn't elongated or squished like some of the others it was... this is hard to describe, but somehow she painted this man looking transparent. And even so it was clear he was middle-aged with brown eyes and brown hair. And it was very clear that painting was of me.

At first, the cowboy hat had fooled me. It took me a moment to notice the blue shirt and the bit of a shining silver badge poking up at the bottom edge of the painting.

Each painting said something about the person. Annie's jealousy, Smitty's conflicted pain, Lila's kindness masking sorrow, and mine... I really didn't know what she was getting at.

"What do you think?" she asked quietly.

I knew Patty painted. When she was in Carterville, she did

Northern Arizona landscapes and lots of Carterville scenes, sold them at one of the local galleries. She was a very good painter, but these were something else entirely. These were Art with a capital "A."

Not that her landscapes weren't art, they were, but these had taken her somewhere different, somewhere deeper.

"I… They…" I stammered.

"It's too much," she said, marching over to the painting of me. "I should have put them away."

"No," I said, and it came out a little too harsh. "They are amazing, Patty. I'm just having trouble finding the words. That's how amazing they are."

"Really?" she asked. She turned to face me, a shy smile on her face. "You think so?"

Patty was immensely talented and skilled, but like most artists she had trouble believing in herself. Hell, that goes for most humans. It's the ones that don't have any trouble believing in themselves that you have to watch out for.

My eyes found the painting of Smitty, the right side of his mouth curled up smugly. Case in point.

"I do," I said, nodding to Annie's painting. "Don't ever let Annie see that."

Patty smiled. "Oh, I know. Believe me. These are all for my private collection. Not tourist fare."

I tried to look at the lake, but my eyes kept being drawn back to the paintings. These were the characters that used to inhabit my world but with more of their true selves showing. This was the world I had been forced to leave behind.

Patty watched quietly and I ended up staring at the painting of the transparent man in a cowboy hat. The painting of me.

What could that mean? That I was see-through, that I was unknowable, that I hid behind my job, that I was…

"I should have put that one away, at least," she said.

I shook my head. "No, no." I turned to her and smiled. "If this is how you see me, I'd like to understand."

She smiled and shrugged. "It's not like I had a plan when I started painting," she said. "I just started painting."

"But by now, you've surely thought about it," I said.

She smiled and nodded. "Yes. I think it's about how you became your job. How the land, the town, made you what you are."

I nodded and looked back at the painting. That was certainly fair, but there seemed to be more to it than that. The proportions of my face, as well as you could see it, were not altered like the rest.

I forced myself to stop staring at the paintings. There were a few more too, one of them, of a young blond-haired woman, the painting yet unfinished. Brooke Jennings.

It was hard to focus, but I had long practice putting aside my own stuff to focus on the work at hand.

I have opined on how a job can make you more than you thought you could be if you let it. And, actually, that was the case for most any job if you really did it. It would shape you in ways you never imagined.

But I hadn't had a job for the past nine months. My self-assigned job was to write about what had happened and that had changed me. I had learned a lot, but there with Patty I was back to doing my old job and it felt good.

Well… it did feel good to have work to do that I understood, that I had done for so long, but it felt awkward too. I was out of practice and doing it here with Patty made me feel self-conscious.

But I had a job to do, so I started doing it. I walked the great room, peered up the stairs at the loft bedroom, examined the sliding glass door that led to a small deck and had a dowel in the track to keep it closed tight. I looked at the high vaulted ceilings with big beams and tongue-and-groove wood. I nodded to the railing of the loft—there was a small camera pointing down, one of those wireless ones you can get anywhere these days.

"I have evidence," she said. "Of what is happening."

I nodded. "Let's see it, then."

FIVE

THE VIDEO PLAYING ON PATTY'S LAPTOP WAS A DARK AND grainy view of the great room we were sitting in, shot from the loft railing above us. The only illumination was moonlight flooding in the windows.

We were sitting close together on the couch and my nose was full of her soapy scent and my body was distracted by her closeness.

The paintings were there on the video too, the Carterville gallery of characters, and it kind of felt like they were all watching me, like they all had something to say.

I'm sure if Smitty and Annie were here, they would have tons to say. And Mary Reilly, if she was alive, had many things she had never said to me. Too many things.

But that was the distraction. That wasn't this job. It didn't take long, and in the grainy video it was hard to see, but the dowel in the track of the sliding glass door silently rose up. Well, one end of it did, the end blocking the door. And then the door started rolling back. It only got a few inches open until the raised dowel stopped it.

The video was still for about thirty seconds, or as still as a grainy video can be, and then, at the edge of the image, where one of the paintings were, the canvas floated up and seemed to turn itself around.

It was eerie as hell. Only an edge of the canvas was in the picture, but after seeing what happened to the door it was startling.

"See," Patty whispered as if she was worried we would be overheard. She leaned closer to me, becoming even more distracting. "The house is haunted."

"Play it again, please," I said.

She did and it really did look like some invisible force raised the dowel and then opened the door. This wasn't Carterville. No one had powers around here. And I didn't believe in ghosts.

"One more time," I said.

Patty nodded and played it again. It was too grainy to see much detail and I started to have this tight feeling in the pit of my stomach. If there weren't ghosts, someone was going through a hell of a lot of trouble to freak Patty out and that scared me.

"I've examined the door," she said. "Many times. Every time. But there's nothing there. Nothing that would do this." She snapped the laptop closed and stared at me like she thought I was Sherlock Holmes and already had it all figured out. I had ideas, to be sure, but they all seemed a little wild so far.

"Tell me more about how you ended up with this house," I

said, once again itching to have a little notebook in my hand so I could look away from those green eyes of hers.

It wasn't the fear in her eyes that made me want to look away, but the need. Patty needed me. Perhaps not in the way that boyish part of me hoped for, but still it was need, and that made it hard to focus.

Her brow furrowed briefly and then she nodded. "This was my aunt and uncle's getaway home. They bought it back in the eighties, drove down from Denver a lot. After they retired, after my aunt died, my uncle sold everything in Denver and moved down here."

She shrugged. "No kids. We were close. He left me the house a couple of years ago when he died."

I nodded. "I remember. The funeral was in Denver, you drove up from Carterville for it."

She nodded.

"But you never said you had inherited anything," I said, keeping my tone even. I was, frankly, a little surprised that she hadn't said anything. I had thought we were close even though we had never managed to do anything about "us."

She looked down, her hands clasped. "I… I was thinking of leaving Carterville. Even before… you know. I just… I don't know. I think all those years of knowing what everyone else wanted left me feeling isolated in my own wants, my own needs. I needed this to be just for me."

I turned and looked out at the lake, a raft of ducks paddling by, a few white clouds in the blue sky. It was an odd house, but perfect for an artist with such great light, such an inspiring view.

"Imagine it, Henry," she said, her voice hushed. I was still looking at the lake and I kept it that way. "Every person you meet is, in some ways, like your best friend. You know everything they want, you feel it secondhand, so much so that you begin to not have any idea what you want. Every day was like I was having a hundred intimate conversations without saying anything and that left me little to give those I cared about the most."

"So, a place that was just yours," I said, "a place without powers, was something you wanted to keep for yourself."

"Yes," she said.

I turned and smiled. "I understand. I was never off the clock in Carterville. Everyone thought they knew me, knew my business, knew my weaknesses."

"I really know you, Henry," she said, her voice barely above a whisper, her eyes darting to the painting of me.

I nodded. "You do. And I know this is probably not the right time or place, but maybe this intimacy overload you are talking about is why you and I… why we never…" I ended in a shrug.

She pursed her lips, looked down at her hands again, and nodded.

This was starting to feel like closure to me, closure between me and Patty. We were having the conversation we should have had long ago but never did.

It all made me hate closure.

SIX

I might as well get this out of the way because many of you are already thinking it. Rare lake-front property and an apparent haunting made me think that someone wanted the property and wanted it cheap.

That is what I was thinking until I saw the video. I had no explanation for what I saw. The dowel raising. The painting moving. If we were back in Carterville, I would be asking Annabelle Unger to look through her database of powers and find those that can levitate, which would have been pretty amusing because that was her power.

If this was Carterville, that is what Annabelle would have done and the flow of the case would have been straightforward. Go interview those that could levitate things and try to suss out a motive, try to find out who had opportunity.

Patty was still on the couch clutching her closed laptop and I was squatting in front of the sliding glass door, my knees complaining loudly.

Fifty-something knees are no fun, which makes we wonder about the future if I'm lucky enough to have seventy-something knees.

I wasn't touching anything, just looking, letting my eyes wander. The metal was old, the black coating starting to wear in the track here and there and showing steel. The dowel was round and plain and fit perfectly in the track. The door had a simple latch that locked it, not particularly effective, but that's what the dowel was for.

"Do you lock it?" I asked, not looking at Patty.

"Every night," she said.

I looked at her and asked, "Mind if I open it?"

"Please," she said.

There was a little space between the dowel and the door, and I gently lifted it. It came clear easily and was just an old piece of wood, worn and scuffed from long use.

I stood up, my knees creaking, and tried to slide the door open. It moved, just a little bit, the latch catching and holding.

I closed the door, flipped the latch, and it slid easily open. So easily that it banged into the other end of the track.

"Wow," I said. "That is one well-oiled door."

Patty nodded. "Kent, the guy next door, is quite the handyman. He looked after things for my uncle when he couldn't anymore."

I had noticed a similar-era house next door when we pulled in. Two story, dark wood, garage out front, except this house had an actual front door.

I carefully slid the door closed, flipped the latch, and tried it again. It held just fine. I examined the door slowly and carefully, even put my reading glasses on so I could see it clearly and could only conclude that it was just an unusually well-oiled sliding glass door.

"What do you think?" Patty asked.

"I think I'm sleeping on your couch tonight," I said. "If you don't mind."

She shook her head. "Of course not. But it doesn't happen every night."

I shrugged. "Then I guess I'm sleeping on your couch until it does happen."

SEVEN

Solving a mystery is satisfying in a way that is so primal, that it makes me wonder if there's something very basic and essential to human nature driving it. But being in the middle of a mystery is tense and annoying, especially when the stakes are high.

And, I guess, the stakes here weren't really that high. Patty's peace of mind was at risk, but, so far, there had been no danger to her physical well-being. But this being Patty and this being our chance to reconnect, it felt like the stakes were high to me.

I was in the middle of the mystery, the point where it feels like there is no possible explanation, and it was annoying and confusing.

That boyish part of me wanted to impress Patty with my finely honed detective skills and my sharp intellect.

Except my success as a detective is way more about persistence than brilliance, and experience. I had been on the job a long time and Carterville was never short on mysteries.

The other thing that I had learned was that if the pieces don't fit together, then you are missing a piece or you are looking at things the wrong way.

I wasn't willing to accept that ghosts were real.

No, let me take that back. Maybe ghosts are real, I had something of an experience when I briefly died in Carterville that seemed like it could have been along those lines, or just my dying brain messing with me. I really don't have a clue about the afterlife, if there is such a thing, but if there is, I don't think ghosts are here opening a sliding glass door and moving paintings.

Taking ghosts off the table, there was no apparent logical physical explanation either, which left me with pieces that didn't fit together.

"Thanks for coming," Patty said with a bright smile, raising a glass of beer.

We had made sure her camera was running, locked up her lake house, and headed to a local brew pub. We were outside on a covered patio, the June air starting to get cool as some guy did a decent rendition of a Clint Black song.

"Any time," I said, raising my glass and clinking it against hers.

I took a sip, and it was strong and hoppy and ice cold. I've never been much of a beer drinker. I got hooked on gin at a young age, something my father introduced me to when I was seventeen, but since I left Carterville, I hadn't been drinking very much. Gin always reminded me of juniper trees and that just made me think of Carterville, so beer was a better bet.

"Tell me about your neighbor," I said.

Her brow furrowed. "Kent?" she asked. "Why?"

I furrowed my own brow and put two fingers to my right temple. "I'm… I'm getting an impression. A… a need. This Kent tried to buy your house after your uncle died."

I was just fooling around, trying to lighten the mood a little, and letting my instincts have the rein.

Her mouth dropped open and she just stared at me. I leaned back and laughed and took another sip of beer. I had only half expected to be right. It felt good to laugh, I hadn't done it very much lately.

"Explain," Patty said, her lips pursed.

I wasn't a psychic, not even in Carterville, so Patty's reaction was understandable. This was serious to her, and I seemed to be making light of it.

"Am I right?" I asked. "Did he try to buy the house?"

She frowned and nodded. "Yes, but he wanted it cheap."

Since I got the first part right, I put my fingers to my temple again, scrunching my face into a look of deep concentration, and said, "You… You hired a realtor. You put the house on the market. But things kept happening. Mysterious things. Things that scared buyers off."

"Jesus, Henry," she said. "What are you doing?"

"Am I right?" I asked.

She nodded.

"Why did you try to sell it?" I asked. "Earlier you said you had been thinking of leaving Carterville before things went bad."

She nodded and sighed. "I had been. But…" she looked away. The restaurant was on a busy street—for Pagosa Springs. To the east the sky was just starting to darken as the sun neared the horizon in the west. There were lights strung above the patio where we were seated, and the sound of other conversations and that Clint Black song washed over us.

"What?" I asked, keeping my voice gentle.

"Lila," she said.

I nodded. She didn't need to say more, and I really didn't want her to. After Lila Chang's murder, Annie and I had broken up for good and it seemed Patty must have decided to stay in case that thing between us turned into something.

"Shit," I said.

"Sorry," she said.

"You didn't say anything," I said.

She shook her head. "I'm sorry," she said, leaning forward. "I had everyone's needs in my head all day long, can you understand how hard it was for me to get in touch with my own, much less express them?"

I nodded. "I can. But..."

"I know," she said.

I'm sure this didn't seem like much of a conversation to anyone that was listening, but between the two of us it was as clear as it could be. There had been a window between when Lila was murdered and when I was ousted from Carterville, a window for the two of us, and that window was now closed.

Because of our powers, she couldn't express her need and I was afraid of commitment and the promises it brought, more than the American male average, by a long shot.

I am human, so I know regret, but what I felt there while the singer strummed his guitar and the cars drove by and the waiters and waitresses carried food around us was way above my usual level of regret.

My job as chief of police was hard. I made plenty of mistakes. One time that led to Lila Chang's death. This new regret about Patty wasn't that strong, but it was newer and fresher. It hurt.

"Shit," I said again. What else could I say? I couldn't turn back time. That was just science fiction. You couldn't even do that in Carterville, at least not that I know of.

We were silent for a while and I kind of remember clapping numbly after the singer was done and sipping a little more of the beer, but I was barely there.

Which was stupid. This was time with Patty, and I was wasting it. The window for "us" may have been closed but she was here. Right now. Carterville was a state away.

When I came back to myself, there was a burger in front of me, but I wasn't that hungry anymore.

"I'm sorry," I said. It was all I could say. Life, in some ways, is the opportunities we take advantage of and the ones we miss.

"Me too," she said with a smile that was devoid of joy and full of pain.

I just stared at her. "No," I said. "I really am sorry. I wish our story could have turned out differently."

She nodded. "I hear you, Henry. The past is the past. It's what we do now that counts."

I tried to smile, but I think it probably looked more painful than hers. "And now we are looking into your..." I looked around but no one was close. "Into your *challenges.*"

She nodded, as if clearing her head, and said, "So explain that whole psychic thing, please."

I shrugged. "Just a guess," I said. "If someone is doing this to you, it makes sense that they would be close."

"But you never even met Kent," she said.

"No, but he has motive and opportunity," I said. "He has had access to the house for a long time."

"Why does that matter?" she asked.

It felt like I was making this up as I went. And I was, but it was informed by long experience, many crimes investigated, and many strange mysteries solved.

I stared at the salad next to my burger. I really wanted the fries. I really hated eating healthy… or healthier, at least, but I was old enough that what I ate really mattered.

I looked up at Patty and said, "He had access long enough to turn your home into a haunted house."

Her brow furrowed and she looked away, out to the darkening sky. I could see it in her face—she couldn't handle another betrayal from someone close to her. "No," she said softly. "Kent has been so kind. No."

Patty had hit her limit, that was clear, so I said, "You're probably right. I don't have much information yet and I was letting my imagination get the best of me."

She looked back at me and nodded shyly.

Part of her knew I was lying but another part of her needed me to lie.

EIGHT

I remember going to Disneyland as a kid and loving the haunted house, especially the ghost that is in the car with you when you look in the mirror at the end. It was delightfully surprising and frightening. It was an illusion, but one so novel, so surprising that it really worked.

It was just a trick of the mirror, but in the moment that didn't matter. The wonder of it was all that mattered. And as a kid in Disneyland, I was there for the wonder. I was there to be wowed. Which is to say, that with illusions, the participant plays an active role in it. Illusions often don't work if you're not wanting them to.

I took my own son to Disneyland when he was eight and the delight in looking in that mirror was watching the look on his face when he saw the ghost. I was older, I was harder to delight and more cynical, I knew how the trick worked, but Tom didn't. Tom was fully there and, for a moment, believing a ghost was right there with us.

I'm not saying that Patty was childlike but that she was participating in the illusion of her house being haunted. There were things happening, to be sure, but she was making it a reality, she was making the illusion real. But I couldn't tell her that. I had to show her how the trick worked so she could see through the illusion herself.

But first, I had to see through the illusion. The difference between the two of us was that I was cynical enough to not believe in it.

After dinner, Patty and I ignored why I was there and sat under the bright stars at the brew pub and talked about the past, about Carterville, about the people and their powers.

She took us there by asking about Annabelle Unger and then Isabella Ortega, the two women that had worked with me at the Carterville Police Department. They were still there, but I wasn't.

"You talk to them, right?" Patty asked. Which made it clear that she didn't.

I nodded. "Pretty often," I said. "Still plenty of strange things happening there."

"I heard Smitty might be coming back," she said. I knew she talked to Frank Paulson, my best friend and the owner of the Carterville Diner where she used to work.

I nodded, shifting in my chair. In some ways, I knew she had turned the conversation to Carterville so we wouldn't talk about her current problem and my uncomfortable theory. This wasn't really something I wanted to talk about, but I thought it might be good for me.

"He was there for a while," I said. "Under house arrest while he awaited his trial. I'm sure you read about the trial and his conviction—it was all over the papers. He's in prison now but I don't think that will last."

"Didn't he get a ten-year sentence?" she asked, her hand absently straying to her throat for a moment before she quickly pulled it down.

I nodded. "He did. And Annie got eight years. But the rumor is that the governor is thinking about commuting Smitty's sentence."

She nodded slowly. "That wouldn't be a surprise, would it?"

"No," I said. "A promise to heal someone he loves or to make the governor feel like a young man again…" I shrugged. "He'll be back in Carterville before too long. And I'll be surprised if he doesn't just addict the governor to his powers and…"

I trailed off because it was too much. Smitty, after all his crimes, was going to go back to Carterville because of his power. And because of my power and the promise I made to him to save Frank, I couldn't.

That left us in an awkward space. Patty didn't want to talk about her "haunting" and I was haunted by the past.

We were both silent for a while, sipping our beers and pretending to be completely engaged with the singer who was now doing an old Eagles song.

"You want to go back, don't you?" she said when the set ended and the singer took a break.

I nodded. "And you do not."

She nodded.

"But how?" she asked.

I shrugged. "The only way I know that will work is for

Smitty to release me from my promise, but he's not going to do that."

Her brow furrowed and she got a faraway look in her eyes. "I'm not so sure about that."

I was suddenly awake, like a hungry wolf that had caught the scent of its prey. "You can't leave it at that," I said.

She smiled and it was almost like the old Patty, and I was even more awake. "It's just a thought. Just a glimmer. Let's deal with what's going on at the house first."

"Okay," I said, and it was everything I could do to not stand up and drag her back to the house.

NINE

Since we aren't there, Patty doesn't have a Carterville "power" but she has power, if you know what I mean. Her mere presence has power over me, but that's not what I'm talking about. It's more the everyday powers that we all have, our strengths that are above average, the things that set us apart.

All of those that were in Carterville eight years ago when the meteor hit were gifted—or cursed, depending on your point of view—with powers that expanded aspects of what they already were. Smitty was something of a conman and his healing superpower made him more of that. Patty was always empathetic, and the meteor just amplified that.

Patty wasn't in Carterville anymore, but she was empathetic and she had felt Smitty's needs many times, so when she said that there might be a way, I believed her.

Which explained how I ended up crawling under her house at nine o'clock at night after a long day on the road with a flashlight clenched in my mouth and a belly full of beer.

Calling this a "crawl" space was, literally, correct. It wasn't tall enough to sit up, much less stand. It was damp and musty, littered with bits of wire, some metal conduit, and tufts of insulation, the kind of crap that gets left behind when someone works under a house.

Our homes are a bit of an illusion too. They hide the wires and the pipes and the messy realities of modern human dwellings. Underneath, it's all there and exposed, out in the open. It's always a little startling to realize the reality of our homes that we cover with carpet, sheetrock, and paint.

The land sloped down towards the lake, so the part of the house I needed to be under, where the sliding glass door was, wasn't that horrible and I didn't need to crawl that far, but my age and my fatigue made it seem both horrible and far.

When I got there, I lay on my back with a grunt and started searching. I had to move away some insulation to find it, but it didn't take long.

I found a blue plastic box about the size of my fist right under where the sliding glass door was. There was what looked like some new Romex wire running to it.

"Got it!" I said, more to myself than to Patty, although I knew she was up there.

"Got what?" she asked, her voice muffled through the floor.

And that was a good question. Was I leaping to conclusions? No, the coincidence was too strong. Weird things were happening under the house and this thing just happened to be there.

As I studied it, I realized it was a plastic electrical box, the kind you would use when installing a switch or a plug into a wall, except this was oriented so the open part of it met the floor. And it looked fairly new, and I was pretty sure that this kind of electrical box wasn't used when this house was built.

"Something that shouldn't be here," I said.

The box was screwed into the floor so I pulled out the Leatherman sheathed on my belt—what can I say, I'm used to having my tools strapped to me at all times—and started unscrewing it.

Inside was a small motor, a stiff wire that went into the floor, and some other small electrical components I couldn't identify.

I'm not an electrician. The extent of my knowledge has been gleaned by working on cars, older cars, but it seemed to me that the unidentified bits were likely some kind of receiver so this could be triggered remotely.

There was no moment of smug, self-satisfaction. I was very uncomfortable, and the damp, musty smell was starting to get to me. But I knew this was it.

"Lock the door and put the dowel in," I shouted.

"Done," Patty shouted back a moment later.

I didn't know a lot about electronics, but I knew enough to "hot wire" the thing, in other words, cross the wires on what I thought was the receiver and switch.

It took a bit, I had to reconfigure the multi-tool a couple of times, but then I shouted, "Watch. Tell me what happens."

"Ready," she shouted back.

I had clipped out what I thought was a receiver and twisted the two wires together. The little motor kicked in and there was a whirring sound.

"Shit!" Patty said. She sounded angry.

"What?" I called.

"The dowel. It's lifting."

TEN

It took a little while and a few more trips under the house, but we figured it out. There were actually three boxes, not one. I had missed the second and third boxes.

The first one used that motor and a thin, stiff piece of wire to raise the dowel. There was a small hole in the track that had been hard for my middle-aged eyes to see, but afterward we found it.

That part was simple enough. The wire lifted the dowel a few inches.

The rest of it was more complicated and, even though it was late, I disassembled the sliding glass door's latch. It's just a metal plate on the house side of the door that has a hole that the door latches into. I found a thin cable attached to it that ran down into the floor. Below it was another box.

This contraption, basically, pulled down the metal plate and unlatched the door.

The third piece of this was in the wall, in what used to be

an outlet but was covered by one of those "blanks" used when covering up a hole like that. It had a bigger motor and round piece of rubber-tipped metal that pushed the unlatched, well-oiled door open. When it wasn't operating, the rubber tip just showed at the bottom of the track and I had thought it was to stop the door from slamming too hard.

Patty and I didn't talk much while we were doing this. After she saw the dowel lift, after we found the hole for the wire to poke up, she got a grim look on her face and went and made coffee while I hunted for more.

The illusion of a ghost haunting the house was shattered, but that's not a comfortable thing. "Shattered" is the right word because it also, in just a moment, evaporated the trust she had in her neighbor.

It's not fun when our illusions crumble, but it's usually healthy in the long run. Reality often isn't what we want, but it's our misperception of reality that causes us so many problems.

As I was disassembling things, I had to admire the work. It was neat and clean, subtle and well done. There was a high degree of craftsmanship at play here—too bad it had been directed this way.

I have found that criminals, successful ones, are often craftsmen. They care about the quality of their work even if all their energies run counter to the flow of civilized society.

"Why?" Patty asked, shaking her head. We were seated in her great room at a small, round, wooden table, the Carterville portraits looking like they were staring at me again. "Why would he go through all of this?"

I shrugged. "Greed," I said. "He wanted the house cheap. My guess is that he was playing a long game with this 'haunted house' thing. After you sold it to him, he would flip it for a nice profit, maybe even rig it for more extensive haunting, and then buy it back cheap when the new owners were driven out."

She nodded and swallowed hard.

The coffee cup in front of me was about half full but the coffee had long gone cold. I was way over my limit for the day and hate cold coffee but almost took a sip for something to do.

It was past midnight, and we were both exhausted, but it's hard to sleep after illusions are shattered and too much coffee is drank. It hadn't taken this long to find all the elements that opened the sliding glass door. Most of that time had been searching the house looking for other things that were out of place. I wanted to make sure there weren't cameras or bugs, that he wasn't watching Patty.

I had found a couple of bugs and pulled the batteries, but no cameras, just the one in the loft, but when Patty told me that Kent had installed it for her, I unplugged it and we changed the Wi-Fi password. There was little doubt that he had been watching.

There could be more. Judging from her description of hearing voices, there might be some speakers hidden in the walls or other hard-to-find places, and the flickering lights could be accomplished with something as simple as a smart bulb. Part of me knew there could be microphones that I had missed, but it was late and I wasn't quite with it.

"Probably bored, too," I said when Patty didn't reply, pushing my coffee away so I wouldn't be tempted. The caffeine buzz was like bees swarming around my tired head. "Small town like this, not a lot to do."

Her green eyes look so sad I just wanted to get up and hug her, but that would have been inappropriate. She sat there, her arms folded, basically hugging herself.

It wasn't just a shattered illusion but betrayal by someone she trusted. Someone close. After Carterville, that had to be hard to take.

"But what about the paintings?" she asked. "You saw it turn itself around."

I was careful to keep my face neutral, remembering the grainy video footage she had showed me, how one of the Carterville portraits, which was only partially in frame, lifted up and turned around. I had a theory, but now wasn't the time to share it. One shattered illusion at a time is plenty.

"Not sure," I said, and I wasn't. With the state Patty was in, a theory was not enough.

"Could…" she began, looking around as if she were afraid we were being watched. "Could that part really be a ghost or…"

I smiled, hoping it looked like a kind, comforting smile, but I was so tired and buzzed-out that I couldn't be sure. I had to guess that in some ways, maybe many ways, Patty missed Carterville and her powers. All power comes with a cost, but it also comes with benefits.

While I had complete empathy for her leaving it behind, I also understood that longing.

"I don't know, Patty," I said. "But maybe we keep with the plan. I sleep on the couch. We figure this out."

She nodded, but it wasn't very believable. She needed more but it's all I had to give.

In the center of the table was a plastic grocery bag with all the components we had removed.

"What do we do about this?" she asked, nodding at the bag.

"Up to you," I said. "We can call the sheriff. I was careful pulling things apart, I'm sure his prints are all over this stuff. Or we can handle this ourselves."

Her right eyebrow raised. "What do you have in mind?"

I shrugged. "He was trying to con you. I think maybe we can con him back a little bit."

She smiled and there was a hunger there I wasn't used to seeing, but there was energy too, which was definitely an improvement.

ELEVEN

In the morning when I woke up, midmorning to be specific, one of the Carterville portraits was turned around. The one of my ex, Annie Smith.

Even with the extremely long day and the very late hour, Patty and I had talked for a while longer, long enough for the caffeine to mostly leave my bloodstream. Even so, I had trouble sleeping. It was the portraits. They were all staring at me with their stretched and exaggerated faces, like they were all accusing me, talking to me about my failures.

I groaned and levered myself up into a sitting position rubbing my face, which sounded a little like sandpaper since I hadn't shaved in a couple of days.

My mouth was thick and sticky, and I suspected my halitosis could be lit like a blowtorch.

Don't get me wrong, middle age has its gifts, but waking up isn't one of them, especially after too long of a day and too much indulging.

It used to be that the indulging had to be extreme and had to be alcohol for me to feel this way. Now it was too much indulging in pretty much anything, even just consciousness.

I smiled when I saw the lake, a raft of ducks swimming by and a fisherman out in a boat about a hundred yards out. Spending most of my life in Carterville, Arizona, I was addicted to views, and this was a good one.

That's when I noticed the turned around painting. At first, I didn't know which one it was, just one of the ones on an easel on the left side of the room.

But then I scanned the other paintings, the other exaggerated faces, and realized by process of elimination that it had to be Annie.

"Shit," I mumbled under my breath.

Patty had her illusion of ghosts, and I had my illusion that all these paintings were staring at me, talking to me. I knew mine was all in my head, my psyche trying to sort through everything, but if Patty saw this, it might deepen her illusion.

I pulled my jeans on and thought about turning the painting around before Patty saw it, mulling it over while I stood up and cinched my belt tight.

This was a moment I always used to hate. It reminded me that I was losing my battle with time, that my hair was receding and going grey and that my belly was protruding more and more.

But that had changed in the last year. My belt was two notches tighter and my belly noticeably smaller. Being out of work had certainly lessened the stress eating and I walked a lot. I was under no illusions that I could win the battle with the years, but at least in this it seemed that I had gained a little ground.

I sighed and took a step forward and stared at the painting. I really wanted to turn it around but that wouldn't be wise. Patty had just found out her neighbor couldn't be trusted and doing anything that might erode her trust in me, even if not acting played into her illusion, was stupid.

And then I heard Annie in my mind. "Well look what the cat drug in. The heart, and goddamn soul, of Carterville itself. And ain't it ironic. You can't go back. And you know what? I think maybe that's a good thing."

It was a little odd. Annie's painting was turned around and yet I could still easily see Patty's exaggerated version of her.

I looked at Smitty's painting and heard a thin nasally chuckle. "Face it, Chief. You lost before you even began. Carterville can live without you, but it can't live without me. I'll be back soon, and you never will."

I knew all these faces and there was something about the exaggerations that Patty did that made them more alive, made it easier for me to hear them.

"Don't listen to them, Henry," Annabelle Unger said from her painting, her southern drawl intact in my mind. Her bright red and purple streaked hair dominated the painting and the colors on her wrinkled face exaggerated her devotion to cosmetics. "They don't know 'nothin. You get on back here, Carterville needs you."

Annie snorted and said, "What she means to say is that she needs you. Why in the world would she stick around if it wasn't for her big ole crush on everyone's favorite chief of police, Henry Carter."

"Shut up, Annie," Annabelle said. "Or I'll shut you up."

"Not before I knock you out," Annie said.

"Oh, is that the way it's gonna be?" Annabelle said. "You

wanna fight with our powers. How high do you think I can levitate you before you put me to sleep?"

In my mind, and in the way Patty had painted them, Annie was jealous and Annabelle was loyal. For the record, I had never imagined that Annabelle had feelings for me, and I can't really say why my mind went there that morning.

Maybe it was Patty and all that had stirred up. Maybe it was the fact that Annie always seemed to be jealous of other women in my life when we were together. Maybe it was my half-awake brain putting some things together. Maybe I was more than a little haunted by what had happened in Carterville, no ghosts required.

"You know what really pisses me off," Annie said to me. "I've been fighting for my life here, I'm going to jail for a damn long time, and not one word of concern, one visit, one lousy letter from the man who claimed to love me."

That one hurt, but this was Annie. She knows how to punch hard, especially when she had the truth on her side. I had had trouble thinking about Annie. The betrayal had been so deep that I hadn't been able to do anything, my thoughts on her going around in circles and then fizzling when something else distracted me.

"Do you really want to go back?" another painting asked in my mind and I was so glad for the distraction.

She was on the right side of the room and I hadn't been paying her much attention. Lila Chang.

Patty had emphasized Lila's round face, jet-black hair, and the sharp line of her bangs that rested at her eyebrows. The chief exaggeration, though, was her brown eyes, big and soulful. In the painting, Lila had a sweet smile on her face, but those oversized eyes told a different story.

I bit my lip and whispered, "I'm sorry, Lila. I failed you."

A lot of the paintings had definite backgrounds, but not Lila's. It was a swirl of colors somehow both chaotic and comforting.

"I know, Chief," she said. "Let that go, will you? You're not the one that stabbed me with a screwdriver on Christmas Eve. Answer my question. Do you really want to go back?"

"It's just not that simple," I said.

"Then explain it," she said.

"I feel lost not being there, somehow incomplete," I said. "Carterville is this little island of civilization dangling on a mountain, overlooking a desert. It feels wrong to not have the mountain in back of me and the desert in front of me. It feels… somehow dangerous. And I fear for the town if Smitty has free rein. I fear for Frank and my sister and everyone I love that still lives there."

"But…" Lila said, gently.

"But if I go back, it will be time to fight again. I'll have to fight just to get there, but if I succeed…" I ended in a shrug. There were no words.

I knew it was all in my mind, but it was too much. I left the paintings behind and went out to the deck to watch the view until Patty got up.

Getting back to Carterville would take a miracle, but being there and standing against Smitty and Karen and their plans for Carterville? How could I possibly be strong enough?

TWELVE

I LEFT THE PAINTINGS AND MY IMAGINED CONVERSATION WITH the faces of Carterville, went through the no-longer haunted sliding glass door, and sat on top of the picnic table on Patty's deck.

I don't know how long it was until Patty brought out two steaming cups of coffee and my phone. The morning was a bit chilly, but I didn't go in to get my jacket. After my conversation with the paintings I wanted the cold, I wanted to wake up.

"You are an angel," I said with a smile that was much lower wattage than I wanted it to be. My cup was only half full, just the way I liked it. Given how many times Patty had served me coffee, it had to be an easy thing for her to remember, but it felt just a little bit like home.

I was sitting on the picnic table and had been enjoying the view, breathing the damp air, watching the ducks and a few folks out fishing.

She nodded and put my phone on the table next to me. "Found it in the kitchen and…" She had a half-quizzical, half-concerned look on her sleepy face. She was dressed in a fluffy green robe that brought out her eyes with some old Ugg boots on and her red hair wild and disheveled.

I had never seen Patty first thing in the morning. I liked it.

And then I remembered the phone.

After Patty had gone to bed and I couldn't get to sleep, I had done some pacing and some thinking. I had fiddled with my phone long enough to find an app that would turn it into a security camera, one that detected motion, and set it up in the kitchen.

Patty's place wasn't tiny but it was very much a cabin. The kitchen was open to the great room with a countertop that doubled as a breakfast bar separating the two. I had plugged my phone in, started the app, and had propped it against a bag of rice I had found in the cupboard.

Given my imagined conversation with the living and the dead of Carterville, I had forgotten about it.

"Set it up to record," I said, holding the hot cup of coffee in my hands, and nodding at the phone.

"Oh," Patty said, looking back to the house. She must have noticed that Annie's painting was turned around, but she didn't say anything. I think we can all be like that with our illusions sometimes. Parts of us know it's not real, but sometimes that same part of us doesn't want to know what is real.

Patty sat on top of the picnic table next to me. Right next to me. Her presence and her warmth were a comfort, but it was also confusing. I had no idea if she meant anything by it. And while I was pretty good at telling when someone was lying—an occupational hazard—I wasn't that good at reading more subtle emotions.

Hell, in this instance, I couldn't even read my own emotions. I cared for Patty, deeply, but we had trauma together and that trauma resulted in the scars on my face and the nightmares I still had about having my hands wrapped around her neck.

"Did you look at it?" she asked quietly.

"No," I said. "Forgot about it."

"You didn't move the painting, did you?" she asked.

"Nope," I said.

She stiffened next to me. Whatever that camera showed it would change things. Deepen the ghost illusion or shatter it.

I wasn't arrogant enough to think that my own conviction about there being a simple, rational explanation for the paintings moving wasn't vulnerable too. Sometimes what we believe is only an illusion in retrospect. Scratch that. Much of the time it's that way.

We were both silent for a moment and I took a sip of the coffee as I stared out over the lake. It was strong and bitter, no cream, no sugar, just coffee like God intended it and I loved it.

There's little in this world better than that first sip of coffee when you are tired and really need it.

"But we're going to watch it," she said quietly, and it was hard to know if she meant it as a question.

"Yeah," I said. "Coffee first."

She leaned her head on my shoulder and I didn't dare move. This was a moment, a little illusion, that I didn't want to end. Patty needed me, and after we watched the video that might not be true anymore.

———

"One thing at a time, Henry," my father used to say to me. I don't think I had ADHD or anything like that, but I was an excitable kid. Curiosity drove it back then. There was so much about the world I wanted to understand.

Like most boys, I was pretty fascinated by trucks and trains and anything big that moved. And the TV, which was a cathode ray tube back then, provided endless fascination. And how did the toaster know when the toast was done and how did a thermos know to keep hot things hot and cold things cold?

The world was full of things to understand, little mysteries to solve, overflowing with wonder.

As you get older, other wonders take over, all revolving around the theme of how us humans can be consistently and persistently so terrible to each other. Society is just a bunch of rules we all made up so we can live in close proximity and not go around trying to kill each other all the time, but the rules we made up aren't fair, and plenty ignore them to get ahead.

Maybe it was that kind of fascination that thrust me into law enforcement. Rules, even if they are flawed, are important. They are needed. We are not benevolent creatures that will consistently do the right thing unless there are checks and balances in play.

For some reason, all of that passed through my head while we were sitting on the picnic table sipping coffee and taking in the view.

I wanted to jump ahead. I wanted to play the video now and get the "mystery of the moving paintings" solved. I wanted to move on to Patty's thoughts on how I might get

Smitty to release me from my promise so I could return to Carterville. I wanted to lean over and kiss Patty while her lovely lips were wet with coffee.

One thing at a time, Henry.

When I was in Carterville, there was so much coming at me so much of the time that I didn't get much space to think. I've had gobs of it since I left and time to think about my father, or have slow mornings just breathing the air.

"You think I'm doing it," Patty said.

I looked at her, but she was staring at the lake. She didn't need to elaborate, she was talking about the moving paintings. Looks like the "one thing" of sipping coffee and staring at the lake was done already and I knew I was going to miss it.

"I do," I said. She needed the truth from me.

"Sleepwalking," she said.

"Something like that," I said. "We went through a lot with that cast of characters."

"I thought of that," she said. "But I never moved the camera so I could be sure."

"Understandable," I said, and it was. Even if she was moving the paintings, she wasn't opening the door. That was the correct initial focus, and after seeing what appeared to be something that was impossible, why move the camera? Why not let it be ghosts and not your own troubled psyche moving the paintings?

"I'm ready to find out," she said quietly.

I nodded and took the last sip of my coffee. Our quiet morning was over. Time to shatter an illusion.

THIRTEEN

The video wasn't very long. The app only recorded when there was movement. Patty and I sat on her couch as I played it.

It wasn't what I thought it would be.

It wasn't a ghost, and it wasn't Patty either.

It was me. I turned the painting around.

I had left a light on in the kitchen to provide some general illumination, and even though the footage was very grainy, the app had done a good job of detecting actual motion.

The timestamp read "02:18 AM" and the video first showed me sitting on the couch staring out towards the lake at the darkness.

I remembered staring at the stars knowing that they weren't in quite the same configuration as above Carterville but annoyingly close.

The paintings were there, the kitchen light reflecting the strange faces of Carterville back at me. They were grainy blobs on the screen, but that night in the dim light they seemed to be even more alive.

The video jumped to 02:24 as I lay down and then it jumped to 04:18 when I got back up again.

Patty stiffened next to me and I said, "What the…"

"Shut up," I said on the video, my voice distant and a bit staticky. "Just shut the hell up, will you? I'm so tired. I just need to sleep. Why won't you let me sleep?"

I did sleepwalk some as a kid, plenty of kids do, but I left that behind with childhood. Or at least I thought I had.

I was standing there in a T-shirt and boxers, my fists on my hips, facing the paintings on the left side of the house where Annie's was.

"You always wanted too much, you know that?" I said. "Nothing was ever enough for you. I was never enough for you. No one could ever be enough for you."

Well, that made it clear—I was talking to the painting of Annie.

"Henry…" Patty said, her voice just above a whisper.

I had thought her illusions would be shattered by this video. I was wrong. That's the problem with us humans, we think we understand far more than we actually do. Rarely do we see the whole picture, and often, when we do, we wished we hadn't.

On the video, my posture changed, my arms crossed and I was shaking my head. "No," I said. "No. That's not true. When we were together, I was with you."

I'm silent on the video for a moment, my head cocked, and then I said, "You're the one that cheated on me. Patty was my friend."

"We don't have too…" Patty began next to me, but I didn't

budge, I just sat there stiffly and stared at my phone. I wanted to stop the video, delete it, but I couldn't. The truth is too important to me, even if it's not what I want. It's that childhood curiosity that I never lost. I want to see reality even if I hate it.

"Attraction happens, Annie," I said on the video. "What counts is that nothing happened. When I was with you, I was with you. Why didn't you ever let me be human?"

Annie always had the ability to give a good tongue lashing. She understood people in ways that often amazed me and never seemed to hesitate to use what she knew as a weapon when she saw fit. And since my inner Annie knew me even better than the real Annie, it looked like I was receiving one hell of a tongue lashing.

On the video, I flinched and stepped back but ran into the couch and fell into a sitting position.

"No," I said on the video. "Shut up. Shut the hell up."

A few seconds later, on the video, I surged up, marched to the painting, turned it around, marched back to the couch, sat back down for a few moments, and then lay down.

The timestamp quickly jumped to "09:38 AM." The picture was bright and clear, the sun having risen. It showed me getting up, pulling my jeans on, and then looking at several different paintings like I was watching a tennis match and then looking at Lila's painting on the right side of the room and saying, "I'm sorry, Lila. I failed you."

I found myself and paused the video. That was way more than enough.

———

Patty and I sat stiffly on the couch, our shoulders nearly touching as long seconds ticked by. I was holding my phone but I really wanted to hurl it across the room. I knew it wasn't logical, but it felt like the damn thing had betrayed me.

"I should store the paintings," Patty said. "I should have done that before you came, but…"

"But you wanted someone else from Carterville to see them," I said, my voice dull.

She didn't say anything, but I could see her nod out of the corner of my eye. I was still staring at the traitorous phone.

"Don't put them away," I said. "We still have a mystery to solve."

"But, Henry," she said, and I could tell she was looking at me now. "This is not good for you."

I chuckled—it was a scary sound. "Better out than in, my old man used to say. I was curious about beer when I was twelve. He took me camping and let me drink as much as I wanted. He kept saying that, 'better out than in,' while I threw it all up."

"Henry…" she said.

I looked at her and almost had to look away. There was pity in those green eyes of hers but also compassion and empathy. She was so beautiful, so close, a part of me wanted to grab her and kiss her and bury all of this under unwise passion. But I wasn't in my twenties anymore, I was in my fifties. I knew better and could feel those things and not act on them.

"To be clear," I said. "The first time I was sleepwalking. I have no memory of it. The second time I was awake. We still don't know how the painting turned around on your video."

She stared at me, bit her lip briefly, and nodded.

"I think we should try to deal with your neighbor today," I said. "Unless you just want to let the sheriff handle it."

"Oh, no," she said. "He pretended to be a friend. Whatever the sheriff would do would not be enough."

I nodded. At least there would be some fun in this day.

Once again, I thought I had this thing figured out. And once again, I was wrong.

FOURTEEN

Our con took a little planning and some time. Patty was engaged and so present, eager even. And I got it, this man had helped care for her uncle, had helped her, had been a constant presence in her life since she got here, and the discovery of the apparatus of the door opening had changed all that. It went from kindness to manipulation, taking this Kent from a neighbor to an enemy.

I made a call to Annabelle and had her overnight me a few things, and then we got in my truck and drove to Durango to hit a few big-box stores. We talked the whole way, working out the plan, getting things straight.

We had unplugged the camera and changed the Wi-Fi password, which I kind of wish we hadn't done now. He would know something was up, something was coming. But it had to be done. There could be other things planted in the house that I hadn't found using the Wi-Fi to help him with his spying and haunting.

It was weird. We had a perp, we were as sure as we could be he had done it, and yet I had never set eyes on him or asked him one question.

After what happened with the video, that gave me pause.

"What if we're wrong," I asked Patty as we cruised down Highway 160 heading east from Durango back towards Pagosa. It was a busy two-lane road that cut through a thick ponderosa pine tree forest, with the occasional passing lane, and the small communities here and there.

"We're not," she said, her voice tight.

"What if we are?" I asked.

Doubt is a terrible thing. I had thought I knew what we would find on that video, but I was wrong, and that led me to wonder what else I was wrong about. Because, being human, there was surely plenty of it.

What was silly in this situation is that this Kent was almost certainly the perp. Motive and opportunity are rarely as clear and as abundant as his. But I had been wrong about something already today and was skittish about being wrong about something else.

Maybe a part of it was not being in Carterville and having the mountain at my back and the desert to gaze upon. Having my team, Annabelle and Ortega, helping me think things through. Patty was great, I was so glad to be spending time with her, but it wasn't the same, and even though Southern Colorado was fairly similar to Northern Arizona, this wasn't Carterville.

Patty sighed and nodded. I glanced at her and she was looking pensively at the forest whipping by as my old truck surged up another grade of this hilly country. "We might be wrong," she said. "Of course we might be wrong. Our plan allows for that." She looked at me, her green eyes intense. "But I'm telling you, we are not wrong."

Confidence is a wonderful thing. It will get you far, help you do things that at first seemed impossible. But too much confidence and you'll burn down your life. There's a line there, and the problem is you never know when you're crossing it. It's a lot like drinking in that way.

FIFTEEN

Patty stared at the brown two-story lake house next to hers as I pulled us in the driveway of her home. If it had been possible to light a place on fire with the heat of a gaze, that house would have been burning down by now. I had known Patty a long time, but this wasn't a part of her I had seen.

Her Prius was in the garage, so I parked the truck in the driveway. Patty had taken a remote for the garage and triggered it.

We walked in and she was about to open the door when I said, "Hold up."

She looked back at me, a quizzical look on her face.

I nodded at the door. "Is the paper still there?"

She blinked and then her mouth formed an "O." She looked at the left side of the door and nodded. "It's there," she said.

I had done the old spy movie trick and put a small piece of paper in next to one of the hinges as we closed the door.

We had wedged the door shut last night with a piece of wood, but I wanted to be able to tell if someone entered while we were gone.

I watched as she opened the door and the paper did fall as expected. After Patty walked in, I stepped in and grabbed the piece of paper off the floor.

"What the hell…" Patty said.

I looked up and even from here, down the hallway, I could see something had changed. My heart started thumping in my chest and I felt a cold, prickly sweat break out on my forehead.

I didn't want to, but I walked slowly down the hallway until I stood right next to Patty and my heart started galloping even faster.

Every painting had been moved except for one. The ones on the easels were turned around, the ones that had been hung were upside down. The one painting that hadn't changed was Annie's, her blue eyes staring out at me.

"Henry," Patty hissed next to me. "This is… What is going on?"

My mind screamed at me that it was really ghosts. That something supernatural was going on. But I didn't believe in ghosts and we weren't in Carterville and there were no powers.

I didn't say a word, my pounding heart loud in my head. I marched over to the sliding-glass door, made sure the dowel was still in the track, and the door was latched tight.

This was a small cabin, there was a window in the downstairs bedroom, so I walked in there and confirmed it was locked tight. I went up into the loft, into Patty's bedroom, and made sure that window was locked.

We had turned the camera up in the loft off so there was no recording of what had happened. The slip of paper was in the door. The windows had all been locked. What the hell was going on?

I came back downstairs and found Patty staring at the round kitchen table, her brow furrowed. "Where is it?" she asked.

"Where is…" I began, but then it clicked. All the gear I had removed had been in a plastic grocery bag in the middle of the table. It was gone.

Well, that chased away any thoughts of ghosts. Someone was messing with us.

Patty opened her mouth to speak, but I put my finger to my lips and looked around. I pulled out my phone and looked for Wi-Fi networks. Patty's was at the top with a very strong signal, but there were three others with good signals. The houses were shoulder-to-shoulder here along the lake and there were a lot of overlapping Wi-Fi networks.

Patty's brow furrowed for a moment but then her eyes went wide as she put it together. She nodded at me, her freckled cheeks flushing red with anger or shame, or maybe both.

Shit.

Silly me, I had thought that by changing the password to Patty's Wi-Fi we were cutting off any other surveillance devices that I hadn't found, but I was wrong. There must be more.

I had told Patty about the paper in the door trick before we had left. That had been heard. Whoever did this had come in through the door and put the paper right back where it was. Whoever did this took all the evidence I had gathered and it was now our word against theirs.

And, yes, I wasn't sure enough of myself anymore to say it was this Kent. I had read enough mysteries, watched enough, solved enough to know that it's often more complicated than that. Maybe Kent was a bit player, manipulated by someone else so that they could get into the house and rig it.

Doubtful, but possible. This wasn't some big-stakes theft. This was someone who was a little bored and a lot twisted who really wanted this house.

I tapped on my phone, switching to the texting app and typed, "We should leave."

Patty pursed her lips and shook her head. "No," she said, her voice strong. "I will not leave my home."

I knew she got the message, but it seemed she didn't care, so I leaned into it. "Maybe this house really is haunted," I said. I was no actor, but I tried to use the stress I was feeling so it sounded natural.

Patty stared at me and I gave her a gentle nod.

"I thought you didn't believe in ghosts," she said.

"I believe in evidence," I said, nodding at the paintings. "I can't explain this. The door wasn't opened. The windows are all locked."

This was something of a long shot. Whoever was listening, and probably watching, knew we had found that the bag of evidence was missing. Might have seen me fiddling with my phone, but that depends on where their cameras were. But it was what I could come up with. If we weren't going to leave, I was going to try to convince them that the "haunting" plan was working.

"And what of the missing parts?" Patty asked, nodding at the table. "Where did they go?"

She wasn't going to make this easy, and that was fine. I could play a part and maybe this would help. "I wish I knew," I said. "I searched this place. I didn't find any more surveillance gear. No one could have known exactly where I put the piece of paper in the door. No one was in here while we were gone."

Clearly I had messed this whole thing up. I had missed at least some listening devices, maybe even a camera or two. Which could certainly be. I was tired last night, and given the access whoever did this had, they could be concealed in ways that couldn't be found, not without the right gear.

I was feeling trapped. I wanted to get the hell out of here, but Patty wasn't following my lead. My face flushed hot and my heart started clanging in my chest. Stinging sweat had prickled up on the back of my neck and my forehead.

This was stupid. Whoever was doing this had listened to our plan. How could we salvage this? I needed to get out. I needed to do something. But I couldn't, so I ignored the paintings, the evocative image of Annie Smith still glaring at me, and stared out at the lake.

There was some wind today so I could see ripples on the water. The sky was blue with a few wisps of clouds.

Patty was staring at me, but I didn't care. I just kept my gaze fixed on the water, pulled in deep, steady breaths, willing my heart to slow down. This wasn't Carterville. We couldn't be dealing with an enemy that could see the future. There had to be a way out of this that brought some justice to the situation and left Patty with her home on the lake.

"Henry…" she said gently. "We… we can leave."

I ignored her and breathed, staring at the lake, feeling my

heartbeat slow. The months away from Carterville had given me a lot of time to rest, but after all that had happened, I found myself subject to panic attacks sometimes.

I felt like a fool every time it happened. I felt weak and useless and embarrassed. The world had just rearranged itself and I certainly had cause to imagine that events were being manipulated around me.

And in fact, they were. Whoever was doing this was pulling strings and had had the upper hand the entire time.

But if I'm being honest, the world hadn't just rearranged itself. The world doesn't do that. It was my perception of the world that had changed, not the world. The world was the world and cared not for what I believed or how I saw it. My perceptions changed the way I viewed the world, the way I was in the world, but it didn't change reality.

What the hell was I thinking in wanting to return to Carterville? To return, I would have to face an enemy that could actually see the future, and here I was not able to deal with a greedy, whacked-out neighbor for Patty.

Patty gently took my arm. "Henry," she said again.

My heart was slowing down and that sick, stinging sweat was receding. "I'm okay," I said. "I just need a minute."

There were three boats on the lake. One with three people and two others with one. I spotted three groups of ducks and a few geese loitering on an expansive well-manicured lawn.

I focused on the details. On the little things.

This was a man-made lake and there were two small floating platforms that kept the water circulating. The fisherman had their lines in seeking fish that had been stocked here.

I was looking pretty much due east, so the bits of mountain that I could see peeking up over the horizon were parts of the vast San Juan range.

These things were real. These were things I knew. These were simple facts.

The ducks didn't care about me or the lake or the mountains or the clouds. So many strings had been pulled to get me out of Carterville that it had left me with a feeling that much of what was happening was about me. That wasn't the case here.

At least I was hoping that wasn't the case. I had been a cop for decades and even with most of it in a quiet, small town, that will leave you with some enemies.

I took a deep breath, straightened up, and looked at Patty. "I need a notebook. A small one. And a pen."

The look of concern on her lovely face multiplied and then a look of recognition melted the concern away. "Like you used to always carry in your back pocket?"

I nodded. "Yes. Time to work this case properly."

I didn't care if we were being listened to. It didn't matter. Anything we had planned today was moot. I had, clearly, been away from the job for too long. I should have started this whole thing like I always do with paper and pen in hand.

SIXTEEN

The notebook Patty came up with wasn't quite right. The size was good, it could fit in my pocket, but it was spiral bound at the top with wire making it uncomfortable when I sat. The pen wasn't right either—it was a fancy blue gel pen, not a black Bic like I was used to.

But that didn't matter, these were my totems.

I know that might sound weird but it's true. Someone younger might make notes on their phone, but that was a multi-use tool that was designed to distract. A notepad and a pen in my pocket were about one thing. Taking notes. Organizing my thoughts. Solving cases.

These didn't feel right, didn't look right, but I eased into it. I wrote Patty's name, the date, and the time at the top of a clean sheet of paper.

"Tell me when the haunting started," I said, the pad in my hand and the pen poised. We were sitting at her small kitchen table.

Patty looked at me, her head cocked. I think she might have been trying to access her power, the one that wasn't there anymore, so that she understood without a doubt what I wanted. But she was still Patty Walsh and she still knew me.

She pursed her lips, nodded, and asked, "For me?"

I nodded.

"The first night I got here," she said. "After I left Carterville, I spent a week in Denver with my sister before I came here. I was glad to be here but nervous being alone. That night I heard some strange noises. But it goes back before that. I had two interested buyers before I left Carterville that said they heard voices and got spooked."

I wrote down a few notes. I printed them neatly and cleanly. If I couldn't understand them down the line, they did me no good.

"What kind of noises did you hear?" I asked.

Patty looked around and said, "But... aren't they..." And then she pointed at her ears.

"Listening?" I asked.

"Yes," she said.

"We must assume so," I said.

She was looking at me strangely and I got it. My mannerisms and tact had changed. I had been the one that had stopped Patty from talking just a few minutes ago.

"Then..." she said, ending in a confused shrug.

I sighed. "I want them to hear this," I said, letting my voice get louder so it would surely carry to any microphone nearby. "They've heard everything else. They know what we were planning so that doesn't make sense anymore. Let them listen to me gathering evidence, properly. Let them listen in when we call the sheriff, let them watch when we have proper gear to find bugs and gather more evidence, let them know that there will be a warrant soon and taking the evidence we found so far will not be nearly enough."

Patty stared at me, blinking.

"So back to my question," I said, looking at my notepad. "What kind of noises did you initially hear?"

———

AN HOUR LATER WHEN I WAS STILL INTERVIEWING PATTY, WE heard a commotion going on outside. A door slamming, the clanging noise of things being hastily thrown into the bed of a truck.

I grinned at Patty and nodded towards her door.

We walked out into the garage, and she triggered the door. Even over the grinding noise of the garage door opening, I heard the unmistakable sound of rubber squealing on pavement.

We rushed under the opening door just in time to see him, Patty's neighbor, Kent. He was at the wheel of an old blue F-150, the windows down. He stopped for a moment and stared at us.

Kent wasn't what I expected.

He was younger, for one thing, somewhere in his thirties, slim with sharp features, blue eyes, and a thick strawberry-blond mustache that was a sharp contrast to his short, thinning hair.

He reminded me quite a bit of Smitty, and that stretched painting Patty had done would work for this guy if you changed the eye and hair color and added a mustache.

I wanted to say something pithy, something that would

qualify as a one-liner in a detective show. But that's not me. I still had my notebook in my hand, so I just slid it in my back pocket, crossed my arms, and stared right back at him.

I could practically feel the heat radiating from Patty. She was furious. Any doubts were now gone and all this rearranging of reality had settled into a bitter betrayal for her.

I know what betrayal feels like, we can't function in this world without trusting others some of the time, and when that trust is turned into a weapon against you it hurts at a very fundamental level.

In reality, reality hadn't changed at all, but the illusion had been stripped away leaving Patty with a much messier, much more dangerous world.

Kent didn't stay there long. Maybe ten seconds. The moment that Patty opened her mouth, to yell at him I assume, he screeched away, the sound of it seeming somehow wrong in this idyllic lake neighborhood.

The two of us stood there long enough so that my nose was filled with the scent of burning rubber.

"What now?" Patty asked, her voice steady but there was an edge to it.

I pulled my notebook out of my pocket and said, "We go back inside and we keep working the case. We find someone around here that has the gear to sniff out the rest of the bugs, cameras, and speakers. We find them all. We get enough so the sheriff can get a search warrant to his house and lock this thing down."

Patty wasn't looking at me—she was staring down the road the way Kent had roared off, her arms tightly crossed.

I was tempted to pull out some platitudes to try to

comfort her, but Patty had just woken up to a major illusion in her life. It was not comfortable, but it was necessary.

"I would like to stay until this all gets sorted out," I said. It wasn't a platitude, it was a promise that she didn't have to go through this alone.

She slowly turned and looked at me. Her face was hard, making her look older than her fifty years. I could see it in her green eyes—she was now having to question me. Wonder if I was who I appeared to be. If she could trust me.

I didn't say anything, I just held her gaze.

Her expression softened and she nodded, apparently deciding that I was who she thought I was, that I was trust-worthy. Maybe sending her my chapters as I wrote them had earned me that, maybe it was the years in Carterville when she knew exactly what I wanted.

"Okay," she said. "Let's get the sonofabitch."

SEVENTEEN

I slept on Patty's couch for five more nights. It took us a while to find the gear we needed to locate the rest of the hidden items, but we did it right. We had a sheriff's deputy with us when we did the search. She took the three bugs, three speakers, and two cameras we found as evidence, pulled the prints, found that they belonged to someone named Lionel Cummings who just so happened to look exactly like Kent Washington.

Lionel was wanted in California for extortion and money laundering, had a juvie record, and had served a stint in Ironwood State Prison in California for grand theft auto.

The warrant to search his house wasn't hard to come by and there was ample evidence there of what he was doing. The deputy assigned to our case found that Kent, aka Lionel, had been running the "haunting scam" on two other houses on the lake.

I could be wrong, but I think that blunted the betrayal part of it for Patty. She wasn't singled out, it was just the scam this guy was doing.

We spent many of those days securing her house. New locks, security cameras you can access from your phone, the whole works.

I worried about it a little. I get that Patty was a woman living alone and such precautions were not without warrant. I just didn't want this idyllic setting to start feeling like a prison. But I supported her, helped install it all, and made sure she knew how to use it.

That left us with one more mystery, the floating painting in the grainy video.

Occam would have loved applying his razor to this problem, and like many human problems, we resist cutting away the improbable because that leaves us with the unwanted probable.

Or at least Patty resisted it, holding on to the probability that it was a ghost or something other supernatural, even when the second painting manipulation had turned out to be a sleepwalking me.

My last night there I woke up and saw a ghost standing in front of the couch staring at the faces of Carterville paintings.

Yes, there was a second bedroom, but I had insisted on the couch for this very reason. If more paintings were to be turned, I wanted to be there for it. Besides, with all the camping I had been doing, a couch seemed like luxury enough.

There was a figure of a woman standing there in the dim starlight that was flooding in the windows. She had dark, curly hair flowing down past her shoulders and she was swaying, her long, diaphanous clothing seeming to move oddly as if there was a breeze that only affected it.

A chill ran down my spine, and if I had been awake enough, I would have thought dark thoughts about Occam and his stupid logic because right then and there I really did believe it was a ghost.

But I was just emerging from consciousness, and even though my heart started galloping in my chest like a spooked horse, I just lay there, trying to reconcile the existence of ghosts as the female form in front of me gently swayed.

My eyes were drawn to a red light up in the corner of the room. That was an infrared camera tied to a motion sensor that I had just installed, the red light indicated it had triggered and was recording.

I hadn't moved, so this was enough to start to break the spell for me. And then the ghostly form in front of me shifted her weight and the floor creaked and all thoughts of ghosts were gone.

I slowly sat up and rubbed my eyes and the ghostly form in front of me resolved into Patty Walsh dimly lit by starlight.

She was still swaying, still looking ghostly, but the illusion was in tatters and I could see reality.

Patty took a step forward and walked to the paintings on easels. She touched the top of Annie's painting and then Smitty's and stopped in front of the painting of the transparent cowboy, the painting of me.

She lifted it up and was speaking to it, but her words were a mumbled whisper and I didn't understand them, and then she put it down.

I was standing, my bare feet on the cool hardwood floor by that point, and I said, "Patty. Wake up, Patty."

I almost didn't. I value truth and, by extension, reality, but some illusions are not worth shattering. But if Patty was going to live here in peace, this was truth she needed to know.

She was still whispering to the painting of me. "Patty," I said louder. "It's time to wake up, Patty. Everything's okay, but you need to wake up."

She continued to whisper so I said in a loud voice as I clapped my hands. "Patty Walsh. Wake up."

She sucked in a sharp breath and said, "What… where…?"

"It's okay, Patty," I said. "I'm right here."

She was still for a moment, and I was afraid she hadn't woken up, and then she shook her head slowly back and forth and said, "Well… shit."

"I feel you," I said from behind her. It had been no fun watching the video of my sleepwalking conversation with the painting of Annie Smith. Waking up in the middle of it had to be worse.

"So, no ghosts," she said quietly. "Only sleepwalkers with Carterville PTSD."

"That's about the size of it," I said.

She turned and faced me. It was dark, and with the starlight behind her she was a vague shadow and I couldn't see her face, but I was painfully aware that I was only wearing an old T-shirt and boxers.

"And you want to go back there," she said.

Her tone was odd and I couldn't tell if it was a question or not, but I took it as one. "I think I have to."

She nodded. "Then let me tell you how," she said. "Now, in the middle of the night and in the dark seems like the right time."

"Thank you," I said.

And then she told me. It wasn't a vague idea but a nearly complete plan. It boiled down to putting Smitty in a similar spot to where he was with the whole "Destroyer of Carterville" mess. Make him so desperate that he has no choice but to turn to me for help that can only be given if I can return to Carterville and investigate. He will have to release me from my promise so that I can help him.

I thought I had understood Smitty, but of course, Patty with her power understood him from the perspective of what he wanted in a whole different way. It made me realize that what we want the most paints a devastatingly accurate picture of what scares us the most.

Patty didn't move as she delivered this information, so I didn't either. I just stood there in my boxers feeling exposed and uncomfortable as the minutes ticked by, my bare feet and my knees complaining from standing so long.

"Understand?" she asked. "Because this is as far as I can go. When the sun comes up, I will not speak of this again and you are on your own."

I nodded, but I wasn't sure she could see me clearly enough so I said, "Understood. Thank you, Patty. I really—"

She held her hand up and cut me off. "Don't thank me, Henry. I am telling you because I know you well enough that you are going to try to go back, even if you have no plan, and you'll just hurt yourself in the attempt, or worse. But I am hoping that now that you know you can go back that you won't have to."

Her words bounced around my head like some kind of weird echo. Was she right? Was knowing I could go back if I really wanted to, if I was willing to pay the price, enough? And if that was true, what kind of person did that make me?

"If you are thinking what I'm thinking you are," Patty said gently as she took a soft step forward, "it only makes you human."

"But…" I began. "You don't have powers here."

She took another step forward and was close enough that I could smell her soapy, flowery scent. "Even without my powers, I know you, Henry. You are one of the good ones because you worry about your own motivations. And you wouldn't be the first human that gave up chasing something right when they knew they could have it if they wanted it. Sometimes we are in it just for the chase."

There was a lot to unpack there. Was she talking about us with that reference to "the chase"?

I opened my mouth to speak but she continued. "And don't think I've done you a favor. You just woke me up and now I just woke you up. Now we both have to face reality."

EIGHTEEN

Patty and I were back in that coffee shop this had all started in, having a breakfast of pastries and coffee.

We were at a table for two along one wall with glossy, high-end photos of the San Juan mountains hanging above us. The place was a lot busier with tables filled and the hissing slurp of the espresso machine going nonstop, the air thickly perfumed with the glorious scent of coffee.

Patty's sleepwalking episode happened at 3 AM. She went back to bed after she had told me how to fool Smitty into letting me return to Carterville. I had just sat down on the couch and stared out those big windows waiting for the sun to crawl up over the San Juans and light up Lake Pagosa.

This left me tired and strung out. The older you get, the more important sleep is. Or, at least, that's the way it's been for me.

Sitting there in the dark, my mind had picked apart Patty's plan over and over again. It had risks. It required a certain degree of moral flexibility. But it seemed to be sound. There was a good chance that I could return to Carterville.

And that left me assessing the cost of returning, examining my motives, and trying to decide what I really wanted in this life. And that's why I couldn't sleep.

It seemed a little late for a midlife crisis, but it had all the hallmarks. I was certainly not young anymore, I was banished from Carterville without a job, and I had to decide what I wanted to make of the rest of my life.

"Don't think about it too much," Patty said over a sip of her coffee. She had some fancy concoction with flavoring and sweetener in a wide, round cup. An abomination, if you ask me, but to each their own.

I blinked and looked at her. I had been staring into my nearly empty cup of plain old coffee ruminating over my ruminations.

"What…?" I said, sounding like I had been half-asleep.

"Don't overthink it, Henry," she said. "Go with your gut. And don't feel bad about manipulating Smitty. He's been doing it to everyone he's known since the moment he was born."

Her tone was light but there was some bitterness laced in there which I wholly concurred with. There are few people on this planet that I felt true hatred for. Smitty was one of them.

"But what about the Fortune Teller?" I asked.

Patty's full lips quirked into a smile. "So, we are not saying her name now?"

I shrugged. That is the name the media gave her. She was the one that architected my ouster from Carterville even though Smitty and Annie had been the ones that executed it.

While I was labeled "Promise Keeper," Patty had been lucky enough to not have so much exposure that she was named.

"Seems best not to invoke her name," I said.

She gave me a tilted-head stare, and then slowly nodded. "Whatever helps you sleep at night."

I had no follow up to that and our conversation had seemed to hit a dead end.

"Sorry," she said with a shake of her head. She pulled her curly, shot-with-grey red hair back into an unruly ponytail. "My choice is clear. I shouldn't project that on you." Her face darkened and she stared down at her coffee. "I'm still figuring out how to be with others without my power."

I nodded and gave her a smile as a thank you. It was, admittedly, awkward being with Patty. Somehow that romantic part of me had thought it would be the same as it had been in Carterville, but that was clearly not possible on so many levels.

"So, what about the Fortune Teller?" I asked.

Patty shrugged. "If you manage to return, she must have seen it. It must be part of the future she was trying to create."

I blinked and stared. It was so obvious. The Fortune Teller has said as much to me when she was caught. She had said, "Yes. As I told you, all outcomes led to my goal. Or at least all outcomes will lead to my goal."

Her goal was to save Carterville. From the "destroyers." From Smitty and me. And her belief was after it was all over that she had achieved that. That all possible futures, or at least the ones she had seen, saved Carterville. And that's why the future she had managed to maneuver us all into was one in which she went to jail. That's how much it meant to her.

"But what if she's just crazy," I said. I had been thinking it, hadn't really meant to say it, but the words slipped out.

Patty's forehead furrowed so I continued. "Seeing all those possible futures, imagining actions she could take to change them, wouldn't that make you crazy?"

Her eyes darted away and she nodded. "I feel crazy enough just trying to be without my power."

"It has to be hard," I said. "My power was not like that. I mostly just hid from it and avoided making promises."

"I knew, by the way," she said. She had been reading my chapters and I had surmised that she knew but hadn't been sure.

"Because I wanted to hide it so much," I said.

She shrugged. "More or less. It's hard to explain how my power worked."

"And now that you don't have your powers," I said, "you'd rather not explain it."

She nodded and took a sip of her overly fancy coffee. "And even though the Fortune Teller is likely crazy," she said, "it doesn't mean that she didn't see your return and factor that into all this madness."

And "madness" is the right word when you are talking about her and about seeing the future.

We sat there, our conversations switching to more mundane topics as we ate our pastries and sipped our coffee. It was pleasant enough but, despite what we had just been through, there was a distance between us.

She was distancing herself from Carterville and I was contemplating returning.

How could I not? Who else would stand up against Smitty and Karen? I felt compelled but I had to wonder if I wanted the same essential thing that Smitty did, and that was to make sure Carterville was the town I thought it should be.

Not that that was possible. I, honestly, thought Carterville would be better off without any powers, reverting back to the sleepy little town it used to be that had been struggling economically.

Part of me, maybe a part of me that was more awake because I was with Patty, wondered what Carterville wanted. Yeah, I know, that's pretty piece of anthropomorphization for a simple guy like me, but do you know what I mean?

Balance is hard to achieve for a human or a town or a country. We get there, to be sure, but only for a moment and then things shift again. It's that balance we all seek. Not too much, not too little, just the right mix of what makes up our life, be it work or relationships or money or responsibility.

If Carterville, the town, were to have a moment of balance, an ideal mix of activities, what would it look like?

Whatever it was, I was pretty damn sure it wasn't Smitty's version of Carterville for one simple reason. Any vision Smitty had about the town was all about him. Smitty was in it for himself, focused on what the town and those around him could do for him. He wasn't there to serve the town like I at least tried to do.

I will admit to biases, mistakes, and failings of all kinds. But every day, I got up and tried to make the town a little bit better. Was my ego involved? Did I get something out of it? Of course, on both counts. I am only human.

"Just go back, Henry," Patty said quietly. "Get Smitty to release you from your promise and go back. You don't have to stay."

I smiled. Even I knew myself well enough to know that if I returned, I couldn't leave the town that bore my name.

She smiled at me and it was a shy thing, like she was suddenly a teenager. "And when you get back there," she said, "if you find out you are truly ready to leave, let me know."

My jaw dropped open, and I just sat there blinking at her. I thought we were past that, that the window of opportunity was long closed, that there was no possible future for us besides friendship.

"You won't be at peace until you get past this," she said. "You know it and I know it. Return to Carterville, Henry Carter."

I could only nod because she was right.

EPILOGUE

I drove west down 160 through the thick ponderosa pine tree forest up and down the undulating hills.

Not far after the scattered homes that were part of the larger Pagosa Spring area evaporated, Chimney Rock poked up above a sharp ridge, and I felt the urge to stop.

It was a national monument, one I had never been to. I wasn't working. I needed to think. Why not stop and look around? The sandstone sentinel that gave the place its name was reason enough, but I had heard it was an amazing archaeological site, the kind of place that would put my struggles into some kind of perspective.

And that's what I needed. Perspective.

But then when the turn came, I found myself unable to do it. This was Colorado and I felt a burning need to be back in Arizona, even if I ended up camping in the desert where it's too hot to get good sleep.

For better or worse I was an Arizonan. The state had birthed me and shaped me, and that's where I belonged.

My hands tightened on the steering wheel as my old Toyota pickup rounded a sharp curve, Chimney Rock already out of sight. Anger bubbled up, and despite the still cool morning and the wind whipping in through the cracked windows, I felt flushed and started to sweat.

Carterville was my home. Smitty had hurt people I loved and used my power against me to force me to leave. I had been a cop almost my entire adult life and I had a hard time dealing with injustice in the first place, but this had been entirely personal.

Patty was right. I shouldn't feel bad about manipulating Smitty. It's not like I would risk anyone's life to do it, like he did to get rid of me.

But the anger burning through me made it clear that I couldn't make this all about Smitty. Going back to Carterville just to fight a war with him would not be good for the town, but could the war be avoided?

"No," I said aloud as the trees whipped by. "No."

Annie had once called me "the heart, and goddamn soul, of Carterville itself" and not just in my imagined conversation with Patty's painting of her. My ego wanted to believe it, of course, and I knew it was overstated, but there was a grain of truth there. I had been a symbol. I bore the name of my ancestors, the name of the town, and a badge. I served as its chief of police, a visible symbol of civilized society.

And, yes, even then I realized it was a lot. It was too much that I had taken on and was trying to return to, the position I put myself into election after election.

The job was hard, too hard with all the powers going on,

and it would likely kill me some day, but, in many ways, it was that job that made me who I am… or who I was. And that's part of what I was missing. Not just the landscape and the people, but the job itself.

The Fortune Teller be damned, I had to return to Carterville even though there would be a war of sorts between Smitty and me.

Best make it quick. Best do it right and make sure Smitty could never ever return to Carterville. But how? I had spent nine months trying to figure out a way and failing, what was different now?

I was.

The faces of Carterville, the discussion I had with them and Patty had changed me.

I didn't know how, but there had to be a way and I was going to find it.

ACKNOWLEDGMENTS

I guess since this section is all about acknowledgments, I should begin with a confession. In 2023, I launched a Kickstarter campaign for *Destroyer of Carterville*, the second book in the series and the third book written (interesting history there). What I've seen other writers do is write a short story to go along with the campaign as a special backer-only bonus.

I was already thinking about what was next for Henry after *The Blood of Carterville* and had an idea of the general shape of it and saw an opportunity to bridge the two books with a short story.

I had a fun idea about a fake haunting and Henry getting some closure with Patty and sat down to write that short story. As you can see, I failed and wrote a novella instead, something too long for the Kickstarter.

All good. I think it turned out pretty well, but one of the reasons the story got longer was Patty's paintings and how they caused Henry to reflect on what had happened. And this is where the real acknowledgements come in. The idea of Patty's paintings are based on and inspired by the artwork of my dear friend Eileen Westphal. Her art, her series of portraits in particular, are quite amazing and intriguingly expressive, and their inspiration made this a much more interesting story.

And thanks to my beta readers, Roni Hornstein and Peter Klein. This book contemplates how hard it is for us to see our own illusions, and I can tell you that it's also hard for a writer to see their own mistakes, so thanks to Roni, Peter, and my proofreader, Diana Cox, for helping me see them.

Gratitude to my ever supportive wife and first listener (these stories get their first airing when I read them aloud to her) Aleia O'Reilly.

And thanks to you for reading. There's more coming soon in *Return to Carterville*.

WANT MORE CARTERVILLE?

THERE'S MORE CARTERVILLE FOR YOU. *RETURN TO CARTERVILLE* takes immediately after the events in this book as Henry tries to return to the town that bears his name.

The best way to find out when things happen in Carterville is to sign up for my email newsletter at RobertJMc-Carter.com/newsletter. When you subscribe you'll get a free 750+ page ebook, *Bits, Bites, and Rarities: The Worlds of Robert J. McCarter*, that introduces you to my many series, and has four stories you can't read anywhere else!

Or, if you'd like a different kind of mystery, check out my *Walter Anchor, Ghost Detective* series. That's right. A ghost who solves murders. The ebook of the first case, *Detecting Haley*, is free when you sign up for my newsletter.

———

ABOUT THE AUTHOR

Robert J. McCarter is the author of more than ten novels and over a hundred short stories. He is a regular contributor to *Pulphouse Fiction Magazine* and his short fiction has also appeared in *The Saturday Evening Post, Andromeda Spaceways Inflight Magazine, Everyday Fiction,* and numerous anthologies.

Robert writes in a variety of genres from contemporary fantasy to science fiction and just about everything in between. His diverse background–including a career in software engineering, growing up on a ranch riding horses, and acting–colors the stories he tells.

He lives in the mountains of Arizona with his amazing wife and his ridiculously adorable dogs.

Find out more at:
RobertJMcCarter.com

BOOKS BY ROBERT J. MCCARTER

Carterville Mysteries

- **Out of a Christmas Sky**
- **Destroyer of Carterville**
- **The Blood of Carterville**
- **Faces of Carterville**
- **Return to Carterville**

Walter Anchor, Ghost Detective Stories

- **Case 1: Detecting Haley** (also part of *Life After: Stories of Life, Death, and the Places in Between*)
- **Case 2: The Ghost Bride's Gift**
- **Case 3: A Long Hard Fall**
- **Case 4: Death of a Dentist**
- **Case 5: A Hollywood Kind of a Murder**
- **Case 6: The Red Arrow Murders**
- **Unfinished Business: The Cases of Walter Anchor Ghost Detective**

For a complete list of Walter Anchor stories, go to RobertJMcCarter.com/WalterAnchor

Novels in the "Ghost's Memoir" world:

- Shuffled Off: A Ghost's Memoir, Book 1
- Drawing the Dead
- To Be a Fool: A Ghost's Memoir, Book 2

- Of Things Not Seen: A Ghost's Memoir, Book 3
- A Boy, a Girl, and a Ghost

For a complete list the "Ghost's Memoir" novels, go to ShuffledOff.com

The Woody and June versus the Apocalypse Series

Find out more at WoodyAndJune.com

The Neutrinoman and Lightningirl Series

Find out more at Neutrinoman.com

Other Novels:

- Seeing Forever
- Where the Past Belongs: An Angelica and Ash Time Travel Adventure

For a more information, go to RobertJMcCarter.com